Curious George®

Piñata Party

Jorge el curioso y la piñata

LIBRO BILINGÜE EN ESPAÑOL E INGLÉS

**Adaptación de Marcy Goldberg Sacks
y Priya Giri Desai
Adaptación al español de Yanitzia Canetti
Basado en la serie de TV escrita por Craig Miller**

Houghton Mifflin Harcourt
Boston 2009

Adaptation by Marcy Goldberg Sacks and Priya Giri Desai
Spanish adaptation by Yanitzia Canetti
Based on the TV series teleplay written by Craig Miller

For information about permission to reproduce selections from this book, write to
Permissions, Houghton Mifflin Harcourt Company, 215 Park Avenue South, New York, New York 10003.

Library of Congress Cataloging-in-Publication Data is on file.
ISBN-13: 978-0-547-238302

Design by Afsoon Razavi and Marcy Goldberg Sacks

www.houghtonmifflinbooks.com

Printed in Malaysia
TWP 10 9 8 7 6 5 4 3 2

George was having fun.
It was Betsy's birthday party.
There were many new things to see and do.

Jorge se estaba divirtiendo mucho.
Era el cumpleaños de Betsy.
Había muchas cosas que ver y hacer.

George heard a wind chime.
He looked up.
A paper animal hung from a tree.
Up close, it smelled sweet.

Jorge escuchó campanitas de viento.
Miró hacia arriba.
Un animal de papel colgaba de un árbol.
De cerca, olía a caramelo.

4

"That's a piñata," said Betsy.
"There is candy inside."
George had to hit the piñata to get the candy out.

—Es una piñata —dijo Betsy—.
Adentro hay caramelos.
Jorge tenía que pegarle a la piñata para sacar los
caramelos.

George wore a blindfold.
He could not see.
He swung, but he kept missing the piñata.

Jorge se puso una venda.
No podía ver.
Trataba de golpear la piñata pero no la alcanzaba.

Steve had an idea.
"Practice using your other senses," he said.
"Try to follow Charkie with the blindfold on."

A Esteban se le ocurrió una idea.
—Practica usando tus otros sentidos —le dijo—.
Trata de seguir a Charki con la venda puesta.

George could not see.
But he could hear.
George followed the barking.

**Jorge no podía ver.
Pero sí podía oír.
Jorge siguió el ladrido.**

But the city was noisy.
George could not always hear Charkie.
So he used his hands to feel what was around him.

Había mucho ruido en la ciudad.
Jorge no siempre podía oír a Charki.
Así que usó sus manos para sentir lo que había a su alrededor.

Click-click.
Charkie's collar made noise.
George followed the sound.
Charkie hid in the fire station.
George felt cold metal.
It was a truck.
He turned on the hose by mistake!
Everything got very wet.

Clic-clic.
El collar de Charki hizo ruido.
Jorge siguió el sonido.
Charki se escondió en la estación de bomberos.
Jorge sintió el metal frío.
Era un camión.
¡Abrió la manguera sin querer!
Todo quedó completamente mojado.

The firefighters turned off the hose.
Now George could smell a wet dog.
He kept chasing Charkie.

**Los bomberos cerraron la manguera.
Jorge sintió el olor de un perro mojado.
Y fue detrás de Charki.**

Now George felt fur.
Meow! It was his friend Gnocchi.

**Luego Jorge sintió algo peludo.
¡Miau! Era su amigo Ñoqui.**

Mmm . . . George smelled yummy food.
Then he heard Charkie's collar again.

**Mmm… Jorge olió algo rico.
Y oyó el collar de Charki otra vez.**

Click-click! George chased Charkie through
the kitchen.

¡Clic-clic!
Jorge persiguió a Charki por la cocina.

He followed the noisy collar.
Soon there was less city noise.
They were in Endless Park.
George felt wet fur.
He found his doggy friend!

Siguió el ruido del collar.
De pronto oyó menos ruido de ciudad.
Estaban en el Parque Infinito.
Jorge sintió algo húmedo. . .
¡Y encontró a su amigo el perrito!

They went back to the party.
George wanted to swing at the
piñata again.

**Regresaron a la fiesta.
Jorge quiso golpear la piñata otra vez.**

George could not see, so he used his other senses.
He heard the wind chime in the tree.
He felt the grass under his toes.

Como no podía ver, usó sus otros sentidos.
Oyó las campanitas de viento en el árbol.
Sintió la hierba bajo sus patitas.

He also smelled candy.
George moved to the piñata.
BAM!
Candy flew everywhere.
Now George could use his sense of TASTE.
That was the best one to use at a birthday party!

Olió también los caramelos.
Y fue hacia la piñata.
¡PUM!
Los caramelos volaron por todos lados.
Ahora Jorge podía usar su sentido del GUSTO.
¡Era el mejor que podía usar en una fiesta de cumpleaños!

Explore Your World

In the story, George uses his senses to find the piñata. Use your senses in the fun experiments below. You will need an adult to help you put on a blindfold first. Now, no peeking!

SMELL

1. Have an adult place five different foods in separate bowls in front of you. These should be foods that have strong smells, such as garlic, cheese, pickles, and oranges.

2. Lift each bowl up, without touching what is inside, and take a good long sniff.

3. Can you guess which food it is by its odor?

   Record how many you guessed correctly here:

TASTE

1. Have an adult cut up five different foods and place them in separate bowls. These should be foods that have tastes you know, such as grapes, apples, carrots, and cucumbers.

2. Using a fork so you aren't touching the food with your hands, can you guess which foods they are just by tasting them?

3. **Challenge:** Do the same thing with foods you have tasted only once or twice before!

   Record how many you guessed correctly here:

TOUCH

1. Have an adult place five different foods in separate bowls. These should be foods that you can feel and recognize, such as spaghetti, ice cream, uncooked rice, and hard-boiled eggs.

2. Can you guess which foods they are just by touching them?

   Record how many you guessed correctly here:

The next time you go to your favorite park, take a look around you. Where are the trees? Where are the flowers? Make a list of everything you see. Now wear a blindfold, and with the help of a grownup, try to find those things. Use your senses of smell, touch, and hearing to remember where all those objects are. When you're done, take off the blindfold and see how well you did.

Your Senses and You

Fill in the blank with the correct part of your body. Just like George, you use your senses every day!

1. I use my _____ to look at pictures.

2. I use my _____ to smell flowers.

3. I use my _____ to feel a cat's fur.

4. I use my _____ to hear a bell ring.

5. I use my _____ to taste an ice cream cone.

Which sense would you use?

You're in your room playing, and you feel hungry. Your dad is making dinner in the kitchen. How do you know what he is cooking?

You're at the park and you are playing with your friend. How do you know when it's time to go home?